I HERO

ATLANTIS QUEST

BATTLE FOR THE SEAS

Steve Barlow and Steve Skidmore

Illustrated by Jack Lawrence

D0610721

First published in 2014
by Franklin Watts

Text © Steve Barlow and Steve Skidmore 2014
Illustrations by Jack Lawrence © Franklin Watts 2014
Cover design by Jonathan Hair

Franklin Watts
338 Euston Road
London NW1 3BH

Franklin Watts Australia
Level 17/207 Kent Street
Sydney, NSW 2000

A CIP catalogue record for this book
is available from the British Library.

pb ISBN: 978 1 4451 2876 4
ebook ISBN: 978 1 4451 2877 1
Library ebook ISBN: 978 1 4451 2878 8

Printed
Frank

How to be a hero

This book is not like others you may have read. You are the hero of this adventure. It is up to you to make decisions that will affect how the adventure unfolds.

Each section of this book is numbered. At the end of most sections, you will have to make a choice. The choice you make will take you to a different section of the book.

Some of your choices will help you to complete the quest successfully. But choose carefully, some of your decisions could be fatal!

If you fail, then start the adventure again and learn from your mistake.

If you choose correctly you will succeed in your quest.

Don't be a zero, be a hero!

The quest so far...

You are a member of a Special Forces naval unit. You are an expert diver and can pilot submarines of all types. You are a specialist in underwater combat and have taken part in many dangerous missions in all of the world's oceans. Your bravery and skill have won you many medals.

You have been recruited by Admiral Crabbe, leader of ORCA — the Ocean Research Central Agency — a top-secret unit whose mission is to patrol the planet's oceans and deal with any threats to humankind from hostile creatures of the deep. Your quest is to help fight the Atlanteans, a race of amphibians who are determined to destroy humankind.

To help you in your quest you have been given command of the Barracuda, the most advanced submarine in the world. The Mer, another amphibian race, created this amazing machine. The Mer are sworn enemies of the Atlanteans and have an alliance with humankind.

TOP SECRET: ORCA Barracuda

(1) Stunfish launcher —
self-propelled weapons resembling
sunfish that produce a low-frequency
sonic wave to knock out enemy
defences.

(2) Crew cockpit —
where the Barracuda
pilots sit.

(3) Countermeasures —
ultra-fast mini-rockets that
target and destroy enemy
torpedoes.

(4) Water cannon —
fires a super-heated water
jet at close range, which
is hot enough to cut
through metal.

(5) Torpedo tubes —
launch supercavitation
torpedoes with
explosive warheads.

**(6) Sub-aqua
bike bays —**
pods for launching
the sub-aqua bikes.

(7) Propulsion system —
powers the sub through the water.
Also capable of a short "jet boost".

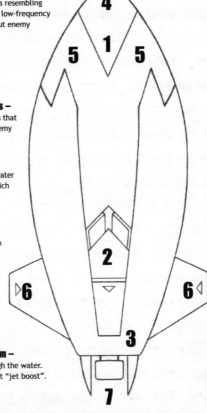

ORCA
ULTRA SECRET BRIEFING DOCUMENT

THE ATLANTEANS:

A race of amphibians, who once lived in the legendary city of Atlantis. Masters of sea-based technology.

HOME:

New Atlantis, a realm under the sea floor.

TRITON: King of the Atlanteans.

OBJECTIVE: To destroy humankind and take over the Earth.

HISTORY:

Hundreds of years ago, the Atlanteans declared war on humans. With the Mer's help they were defeated. Entrance to Atlantis is guarded by the Mer.

BACKGROUND INFORMATION:

The Atlanteans have broken out from New Atlantis. They have declared war on humans and the Mer.

With the help of Shen, a female Mer, you have managed to defeat Hydros, one of Triton's commanders. With the pressure shield generator from Hydros's command ship, the Barracuda can now dive to unlimited depths.

You have also defeated the Atlantean commander Hadal, and salvaged the defensive shield from his ship, giving you greater ability to withstand enemy fire.

Admiral Crabbe has now ordered you to find the gap in the seabed through which the Atlanteans are escaping. You must find a way to send the Atlanteans back and then close this before Triton can carry out his threat to destroy humankind.

The future of the Earth depends on you...

Go to 1.

1

You stare at the Barracuda's detection screens. "There's a lot of ocean floor down there. It will take months to search for where the Atlanteans are escaping."

The detector beeps and Shen points at her screen. "I'm picking up another sub — an Atlantean ship."

You are instantly on the alert. "A warship?"

Shen shakes her head. "No, it looks like a supply vessel. It's leaking fuel and moving slowly. It seems to be damaged."

You give her a grin. "It will be heading to Atlantis for repairs. All we have to do is follow it..."

You are cut off by an urgent voice from the comms. "This is Mer City! We are under attack! Captain Tempest and her forces have launched an all-out assault on our city. We need reinforcements!"

Shen looks stunned. "That's my home! The Atlanteans will destroy it! We must go and help!"

If you agree with Shen that you must help protect Mer City, go to 34.

If you wish to follow the damaged Atlantean vessel, go to 45.

2

"Let me talk to them," you say. You thank the captain for his offer, and ask him how he can help you.

"We are Selkies," says the captain proudly. "Our underwater vehicles are not as powerful as your Barracuda, but we have special senses. We can find things underwater far more easily than Atlanteans and Mer can, no matter how clever their instruments."

"We could work together then. Can you find Captain Tempest's Nautilus?" you ask.

"Certainly," says the Selkie. "Follow my vessel."

The Selkie vessel shoots ahead, and you follow. Before long, you come upon part of the seabed unoccupied by Atlantean forces.

"The Nautilus is there," reports the Selkie captain.

"I can't see anything," you tell him.

"Naturally. The vessel is cloaked."

If you want to attack the Nautilus, go to 19.
If you want to ask Shrim for advice, go to 37.

3

You leave Captain Tempest unconscious on the ground, and hurriedly begin your search for the cloaking device. You have almost completed your search, when Captain Tempest's evil laughter fills the room. You spin round. Tempest is awake again!

"You've been looking in the wrong place,"

she says, before firing her gun at you. The barbed dart catches you in the chest, and you drop to the floor.

You were so close to finding the top-secret cloaking device! Get back to 1 to try again.

4

You find Shen's father, Admiral Merrow, in the Strategic Command Centre organising the defence of Mer City.

Shen introduces you. The look her father gives you is far from friendly. "This attack by

the Atlanteans is what our alliance with ORCA brings us! And now my daughter brings a human into our city! I do not approve. We have had to pump air into this part of the command centre so you can breathe. I can feel my skin drying out already!" He turns to Shen. "You are a Squid warfish pilot. Now that you are here, rejoin your squadron. We need you to help defend the city."

This is bad news! Only Shen knows the Barracuda as well as you do.

If you want to object to Admiral Merrow's decision, go to 17.

If you think Shen should do as her father orders, go to 36.

5

You find yourself in an airtight viewing bubble looking across an underwater cave. Most of the cave is occupied by something that looks like a gigantic brain.

"This is the Brain Coral," says Admiral Merrow. "It is a superintelligent organism that we Merpeople use as an organic CPU for our computers, comms, navigation — and for advice!"

The admiral instructs you to place the cloaking device on a sensor pad in the middle of the floor. Lights flash as the Brain Coral scans the device.

"I can copy this," it announces, "and fit similar devices to all our ships. But there is something more. I calculate that by changing the polarity of this device, it will function, not as a camouflage mechanism, but as its opposite – a detector. It should be possible to use it to find cloaked Atlantean vessels at long range..."

"And if we can do that," you exclaim, "we can find the hole in the ocean floor!"

At that moment, a messenger arrives and salutes the admiral. "Sir!" he says. "I have urgent news."

The messenger takes a deep breath. "Admiral, your daughter – Shen. Her Squid warfish was captured in the battle. One of her squadron saw her being captured and taken onto a Lionfish destroyer."

Admiral Merrow seems to grow old before your eyes. "My daughter," he groans, "in the hands of the enemy!"

To offer to help rescue Shen, go to 9.
If you don't wish to do this, go to 47.

You know that the Selkies will be able to help you see the ship and locate an entrance, so you thank the Selkie captain and take up his offer.

Soon you are thrusting forward in the Barracuda accompanied by two Selkies riding dolphins. At that moment the Selkie subs open up their attack. The Nautilus is hit by several Selkie torpedoes. The Nautilus is distracted and

doesn't seem to detect you. The two Selkie riders point towards where the docking bay doors are. "Activate water cannon," you tell Shrim. The super-hot jet of water cuts into the metal. Soon you've sliced a hole big enough to fit the Barracuda through. You thrust through the gap as the Selkie riders wave goodbye and head back towards their vessels.

You order Shrim to stay with the Barracuda, while you head to the airlock to begin your search.

Go to 42.

7

"Attack!" you order. "Fire torpedoes!"

Your aim is good. Your torpedoes strike both Atlantean subs — but neither one is destroyed. They immediately turn towards the Barracuda and return fire.

"Defensive shields on!" you order.

The Atlantean torpedoes strike the Barracuda. Your vessel is pounded by huge explosions. The cabin lights dim and a red light flashes.

"Defensive shields down," reports the Barracuda's computer voice.

Shen shakes her head. "We're no match for two destroyers — even the defensive shields we took from Commander Hadal's ship aren't strong enough."

Go to 38.

8

You reach the Barracuda. "I've got the cloaking device. Shrim, get it installed. Let's head for the front line and cause some trouble!"

You navigate out of the docking bay while Shrim takes the device and begins work. "Firing torpedoes!" You launch a salvo of torpedoes at the hole you made in the docking bay doors and they detonate, crippling the vessel. "Leave the Selkies to finish off Tempest's ship."

By the time you reach the Atlantean battle group, Shrim reports that the cloaking device is ready.

"Activate cloaking device," you order. The Barracuda turns invisible! Your torpedoes cause

panic in the Atlantean ranks as they suddenly find themselves under attack by an invisible enemy. Without Captain Tempest to lead them, and with their secret weapon turned against them, the Atlanteans flee.

To continue your attack, go to 18.

If you wish to head to Mer City, go to 33.

9

You clench your fists in frustration. "Even if I find the hole where the Atlanteans have broken through, I can't close it with Shen on the other side! She is my friend. I must try to rescue her."

The admiral nods. "You will need help. I will gather a task force."

If you want to wait for the task force to assemble, go to 28.

If you want to get after Shen quickly on your own, go to 50.

10

You know roughly where Tempest is standing, and fire a stun grenade. It misses, but the blast catches her and knocks her down. As Tempest

crashes to the floor, she reappears! You rush over. What did she mean by "I am the secret weapon"?

If you want to search the room for the secret weapon, go to 3.

If you want to search Captain Tempest, go to 40.

11

"Admiral!" you cry. "You say you regret being allied with ORCA — but at least I am ready to fight for you, which is more than these cowards are prepared to do!"

One of the Selkies gives you a cold look. "You accuse us of cowardice? Very well, then our final answer is fight the Atlanteans yourselves!" The creature gathers up his followers, and sweeps out.

Admiral Merrow is furious. "We cannot beat Atlantis without the Selkies' help, and we could have persuaded them to join us! Now you have offended them they will never fight for us." He raises his voice. "Guards! Lock him up!"

You can't help Shen or her people in prison! Go back to 1.

12

You head inside the room. It has been damaged by the Selkie attack, but you can make out a row of screens and a chair. The door slides closed behind you, and you spot something else moving. There is someone in the room with you! You take cover behind the chair, with your jet gun at the ready.

"Silly human," a female voice says gently. "Look how frightened it is — like a little shrimp." You look around, but can't see who is speaking.

"Who are you?" you call out.

"Don't you know? I'm Captain Tempest, Triton's secret weapon!" Suddenly a figure appears right beside you and knocks you to the floor. As you recover, the figure vanishes again. Evil laughter fills the room. Captain Tempest is

the secret weapon — she controls the cloaking device, and can turn herself invisible! A barbed dart pierces the chair. You decide to fire back at where it came from.

If you want to fire an explosive grenade from your jet gun, go to 46.

If you want to fire a dart from your jet gun, go to 35.

13

You radio back to the Selkie Captain.

"I apologise, Captain, for my foolishness earlier, but I do need your help."

"You are too late," replies the captain. "I have just given orders for the attack..."

You look up and see dozens of torpedoes heading for the Nautilus. The Nautilus opens fire too — and the Barracuda is caught right in the middle! You have to get out of here!

Go to 21.

14

You fire at Tempest using your dart gun, but the shot misses again. Suddenly you feel a crushing pressure around your neck. Tempest has you in her grasp, but you still can't see her! You thrash around, until you run out of air. The last thing you hear is Tempest's evil laughter ringing in your ears.

Tempest has won! Go back to 1.

15

You fold your arms. "Well, I'm certainly not taking on the entire Atlantean Navy on my own!"

Admiral Merrow gives you a scornful look. "I always thought humans were cowards — and you have proved me right! I will find someone more worthy to rescue my daughter."

You are horrified. "But I am the captain of the Barracuda..."

"No longer!" snaps Merrow. "Get out of my sight!"

What are you, a minnow? Go back to 1.

16

Some time later, Shen points. "There's the seamount — and there's Mer City!"

You nod. "And it has company."

You tilt the Barracuda so that you have a good view of the seabed.

Mer City is built on top of an underwater mountain, and a mighty Atlantean force is heading across the flat seabed surrounding it.

Shen points out the different Atlantean craft. "Turtle troopships — each one carries a hundred warriors. The things scuttling around them are Crab tanks. They're heavily armoured with lots of firepower. And Ray fighters — we know all about them."

"It looks as if the battle has already started!" you say as a squadron of Merpeople Squid warfish dives down to attack the Atlantean Ray fighters.

You reach the front line of the conflict. Merpeople Trilobite tanks and Horseshoe crawlers are battling Atlantean Crab tanks. You point to small figures darting around the tank formations. "What are those?"

"Atlantean cavalry," says Shen. "They're using cyborg seahorses, and they're engaging the Mer cavalry riding Angelfish PWCs."

You nod. "Personal Water Craft — like

humans use on the surface."

"But much faster and more manoeuvrable."
Shen points to flashes like miniature lightning.
"Both sides are using electric lances."

You shake your head. "It looks as if the Mer
are being pushed back."

Shen clenches her fists. "We have to join
the fight!"

If you agree with Shen, go to 25.

**If you think you should go on to Mer City,
go to 48.**

17

"But, Admiral!" you protest. "Shen is my crew!
And she is an officer of ORCA!"

Merrow is furious. "Shen is under
my command! I did not ask for human
interference, and I will not have my orders
questioned! Is that clear?"

You realise that you have no official position
here. You salute the admiral. "I apologise, sir. I
withdraw my objection."

Go to 36.

18

You continue to fire at the Atlantean ships, until you have almost run out of torpedoes.

As you follow one ship it suddenly drops a row of mines. "Warning! Mines ahead!" the Barracuda says.

You curse — although they couldn't see you, the Atlanteans could lay mines to stop their invisible attacker!

"Taking evasive action!" you order, but you're going too fast. The Barracuda hits a mine, setting off a chain reaction as dozens of mines explode. The Barracuda's defensive shield is destroyed. You limp back to ORCA HQ, unable to carry on your quest.

Go back to 1.

19

"Attack!" you order.

Shrim is horrified. "That's crazy!"

You ignore him. "Firing torpedoes!"

The Nautilus detects you and releases a tidal wave of torpedoes straight towards the Barracuda. "Deploy countermeasures!" you shout. The defensive shield blocks the first wave of torpedoes, but you cannot survive another strike. You do the only thing you can. Run away!

With the Barracuda so badly damaged, you cannot complete the quest. Go back to 1.

20

"We can't take on two destroyers at once," you tell Shen. "Even the defensive shields we took from Commander Hadal's Man-of-war aren't strong enough." You think for a moment. "Steer towards them," you say. "Make it look as if we haven't seen them then the minute they attack, turn and run!"

Shen looks puzzled, but obeys your order.

As soon as the Lionfish destroyers spot the Barracuda, they turn to attack.

"Now!" you cry. "Run!"

You turn and flee, with the Atlantean subs in pursuit. But your screens reveal that one is moving more slowly than the other.

You wait until the second sub is far behind the first. "Now we attack!" you cry.

You swing the Barracuda around and open fire. Both your torpedoes strike the leading destroyer. Bubbles rise and debris spills from its ruptured hull. Its engines stop. The Atlantean vessel hangs dead in the water.

If you wish to finish off the disabled vessel, go to 29.

If you decide to attack the second, slower Lionfish destroyer, go to 41.

21

"Jet boost!" you order the Barracuda.

You spin the super sub around, but you are too late. As the Selkie torpedoes hit the Nautilus, you are caught up in the explosion. The defensive shield protects you, but the Barracuda is badly damaged. You limp back to Mer City, unable to carry on your quest.

Go back to 1.

22

You decide to fire a grenade from your jet gun's launcher. You aim down the corridor and fire. The grenade fizzes through the air and explodes, taking out the enemy in one go.

You hear more explosions and the ship rocks. You speed up, searching for the top-secret cloaking device. After searching several rooms, you are moving down a corridor when a huge blast knocks you to the floor.

To pick yourself up and head through the next door, go to 12.

To scramble to your feet and continue down the corridor, go to 30.

23

You bow to the Selkie ambassador. "Sir," you say, "do you really think that if the Atlanteans defeat the Merpeople, they will leave you alone? My people do not even live under the sea, but they have sent me to join in the fight against Atlantis."

The Selkie gazes at you. "There is much in what you say." He turns to his advisors and holds a muttered conversation.

Then he turns back to you. "Very well. If surface-dwellers are willing to fight, can Selkies do less? We will ally ourselves to the Merpeople."

As he sweeps away, Admiral Merrow smiles. "Well said. You may be of use to us after all. If you are serious about helping us," says Merrow, "I have a task for you."

"Name it!" you say.

Go to 49.

24

You talk to the Selkie captain and explain the situation to him.

"So what do you think we should do?" asks the captain.

"If you Selkies attack the ship it will create a diversion and give me time to get inside the Nautilus and find the cloaking device," you suggest.

"Shall I send some of our people to help you you get inside the ship?" asks the captain.

If you want to take up the captain's offer, go to 6.

If you wish to go on your own, go to 39.

25

"You're right," you say. "Let's go and get them!"

You dive towards the battle, firing torpedoes and your sonic Stunfish weapons at any target that presents itself. Soon, Ray fighters and Crab tanks are falling to your assault.

But you have attracted the Atlanteans' attention. Ray fighters swarm around you. Crab tank turrets swing round to target the Barracuda. Your vessel is rocked by explosions.

Shen checks her instruments. "Our defensive shields are failing. Should we break off the attack?"

To break off the attack, go to 48.
To continue the attack, go to 38.

26

You continue to guide the Barracuda through the water, desperately searching for the Nautilus. The Selkies will soon launch their attack — you have got very little time!

Sudddenly, you see flashes of light as the invisible Nautilus opens fire on you. The Selkie ships arrive, and return fire. You have to get out of here!

Go to 21.

27

"Thanks," you say, "but I'll go alone."

An hour later, you guide the Barracuda back out to sea.

Despite your stealth mode, you are instantly spotted by Atlantean Ray fighters. They swarm around you like wasps, firing torpedoes at you. Sailing alone, you are unable to dodge or return fire effectively. Your defensive shield begins to fail.

The computer beeps in warning. "Shield down. Do you wish to surrender?"

Go to 38.

28

"Thank you," you say, "I'll need a lot of backup."

"Wait!" Admiral Merrow pauses in thought. "We only have one cloaking device. That would protect the Barracuda, but the rest of the task force would be visible. The Atlanteans would see you coming!"

If you wish to insist on backup, go to 15.
If you think the admiral is right, go to 50.

29

"Finish them off!" you snap. "No mercy!"

Shen looks doubtful, but obeys your orders, firing torpedo after torpedo at the stricken destroyer, which begins to break up in the water.

Suddenly, the Barracuda is rocked by a tremendous explosion. You are thrown from your seat. Water squirts from the damaged hull, soaking you. Your ears are ringing. "Where did that come from?"

"The second destroyer!" Shen is desperately wrestling with the controls. "It's caught up with us."

"Defensive shields down," reports the Barracuda.

You struggle back to your seat.

"Should we surrender?" asks Shen.

Go to 38.

30

You head along the corridor when suddenly there is a violent explosion. You are swept up in a massive fireball. Debris crashes down around you, crushing you under its weight.

You have failed to find the top-secret cloaking device. Your quest is over, go back to 1.

31

You don't think Merrow's volunteer will be as good as Shen, but you know that some help is better than none at all. "Thanks," you say, "I'll meet them on board the Barracuda."

An hour later, you are out at sea again with Shrim — your Mer volunteer. He's a young Mer technician from Mer City. You are scanning for

Tempest's ship, without any luck so far. A Selkie submarine comes alongside. Shrim looks up from the radio. "The Selkies want to know if they can help us."

If you wish to accept the Selkies' offer, go to 2.

If you wish to refuse the offer, go to 43.

32

You turn around and try to run away, but several harpoon bolts spear you in the back. You stumble and crash to the ground knowing the end is not far away.

You have failed. Go back to 1.

33

As soon as the Barracuda docks in Mer City, it is surrounded by cheering well-wishers, who raise Shrim up above the crowd in triumph.

Admiral Merrow also appears, and takes your hand in his webbed fingers. He smiles for the first time since you met him. "It is worth the inconvenience of breathing air to welcome you back to our city!"

You thank him. "I have the cloaking device aboard."

"Excellent!" says Merrow. "We must take it to the Brain Coral."

"What is the Brain Coral?" you ask.

"Follow me and see," replies the admiral.

Go to 5.

34

Shen sets a course for Mer City. The Barracuda swings round and speeds up.

You switch your detector screens to search for Atlantean ships. Soon you pick up signals. "There are two vessels in front of us."

Shen checks her screens. "Lionfish destroyers," she says.

Ship type –
Lionfish destroyer –
fast attack vessel.

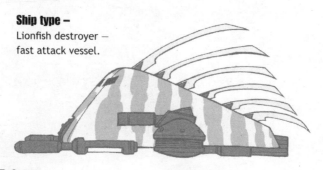

Defence –
Power shockwave generated
by spines on back.

Power system –
Fuel cell propulsion system at rear.

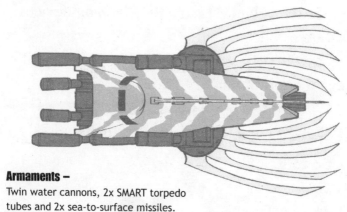

Armaments –
Twin water cannons, 2x SMART torpedo
tubes and 2x sea-to-surface missiles.

"They're fast, heavily armed and very dangerous," Shen continues. "These two are travelling together, quite slowly."

"It could be that one of the Atlantean subs is damaged, and the other is escorting it to safety," you suggest.

"What do you want to do?" asks Shen.

To attack both subs together, go to 7.
To try to separate the subs, go to 20.

35

Even though you can't see Captain Tempest, you fire your dart gun. Your shot misses.

"It's hard to hit what you can't see, isn't it? I'll soon defeat your furry Selkie friends, and then humankind will be next! But first, let's get this over with."

Captain Tempest may be invisible, but you can tell roughly where her voice is coming from.

"You talk too much," you say.

To fire another dart, go to 14.
To fire a stun grenade from your launcher, go to 10.

36

The admiral waves Shen away. She gives you an
apologetic look, and leaves.

A group of strange-looking beings approaches
the admiral. They are shaped like humans, but
have the fur and features of seals.

One steps forward. "Admiral," it says in a soft voice, "I am sorry to say that the Selkie High Command has still not decided on whether to join your fight with Atlantis."

If you think the Selkies are being cowardly, go to 11.

If you want to persuade the Selkies to fight, go to 23.

37

"I don't think we can tackle a thing that size on our own," you say.

"What about calling for ORCA reinforcements?" Shrim suggests.

"By the time they arrive, the Nautilus will have moved," you reply.

If you want to attack anyway, go to 19.

If you want to talk to the Selkies, go to 24.

38

"Continue the attack!" you order.

But a split second later your scanner shows dozens of torpedoes heading straight for the Barracuda.

You know there is no way your vessel can survive such an attack.

The Barracuda is caught in a series of gigantic explosions. The hull splits. The ocean rushes in, sending you to oblivion.

You have paid the ultimate price for your recklessness. Go to 1.

39

"Thanks, but I'll head to the Nautilus myself," you tell the captain. "Begin the attack in five minutes. That should distract Tempest long enough for me to get inside. Then I'll get out with the cloaking device and we can finish off the enemy together!"

You thrust the Barracuda forwards, but you quickly realise that you have made a mistake! Because of the cloaking shield you cannot see the ship, even when you are close to it!

If you wish to continue looking for it, go to 26.

If you want to ask for the Selkies' help, go to 13.

40

Tempest said "I am the secret weapon", so she must have it on her. You search quickly, but can't see anything that could be a controller. You're just about to give up, when you see a flashing light under Tempest's uniform. You open it to reveal a device built into her skin.

It must be the cloaking device! As you turn
the flashing unit to pull it out, Tempest's hand
grabs you! "No!" she shrieks, but it's too late.
The unit comes away and her lifeless hand and
body slump down, dead. With the unit safely
in your grasp, you quickly get to your feet
and race back to the docking bay where the
Barracuda is waiting.

**If you want to head straight back to Mer
City, go to 44.**

**If you decide to install the cloaking device,
go to 8.**

41

Leaving the damaged Lionfish destroyer, you
head for the second, slower Atlantean vessel.

"Fire torpedoes!" you order.

Your torpedoes race towards the enemy sub
and strike. There is an enormous explosion.

Seconds later, there is nothing left of the
destroyer but a cloud of debris.

"It blew up!" says Shen. "Its defence shields
must have been down. We must have hit the
engines — or a weapons store." She turns to

you. "What about the first ship?"

"Leave it," you say. "We have to get to Mer City as soon as we can."

Go to 16.

42

Although the Nautilus is under attack, you know the Selkie ships aren't strong enough to defeat it. You have to get the cloaking device to stop Tempest's assault on Mer City! Armed with your jet gun, you fight your way out of the docking bay to a junction.

As you head towards it, a troop of Atlantean guards turn around the corner.

If you want to get away, go to 32.
To attack the Atlanteans, go to 22.

43

You shake your head. "Tell them, 'thanks, but no thanks'."

The Selkie sub pulls away. Shrim looks puzzled, but says nothing.

After several hours of fruitless searching during which you have been attacked many times, you are no closer to finding the Atlantean captain's vessel.

"We can't stay out here with the amount of damage we've taken," you say. "I'm taking us back to Mer City."

Admiral Merrow is furious. "You've offended our allies, you've failed to find Tempest, and your ship will take days to repair! I've no room on my staff for fools! Get out of my sight!"

If Mer City survives, it will be no thanks to you! Go back to 1.

44

You reach the Barracuda. "I've got the cloaking device. Set a course for Mer City!" Shrim navigates out of the docking bay. "Firing torpedoes!" You launch a salvo of torpedoes at the hole you made in the docking bay doors and they detonate, crippling the vessel. "Leave the Selkies to finish off Tempest's ship."

You quickly reach Mer City — but there's an entire Atlantean battle group between you and the city. They've spotted you and direct their forces towards you. Torpedoes rain down on you, and even with the defensive shield, you have no chance against such overwhelming firepower.

"Systems failing!" Shrim reports, just as the Barracuda implodes.

Go to 1 to try again.

45

You shake your head. "We may never get another chance to find out where the Atlanteans are coming from! Follow that sub. Mer City will have to take care of itself."

Shen stares at you. Her face is hard and unforgiving. "My people built the Barracuda. Now they need it! And they need me! I'm going to Mer City — if you don't want to come, go and get on a sub-aqua bike!"

You realise that Shen is right. "I'm sorry. Set course for Mer City."

Go to 34.

46

You point the grenade launcher in the direction that the dart came from, and pull the trigger. Too late, you realise the danger... The grenade detonates with a huge explosion, instantly killing you and Tempest.

You were crazy to use the grenade launcher in a confined space! Go to 1.

47

You shake your head impatiently. "Admiral, we have no time to waste! Have the cloaking device installed on the Barracuda, and I will set off to find Atlantis. If I can seal the rift in the ocean floor, the Atlanteans will be trapped."

Merrow glares at you. "Captain Tempest's defeated forces will retreat to Atlantis. If you seal the rift now, my daughter will be on the other side!"

"I am sorry about Shen," you say, "but sometimes, sacrifices must be made."

The admiral is furious. "Does Shen mean so little to you? You have fought together — she is your friend! And you would leave her a prisoner in Atlantis — forever!" He calls his guards. "Lock this human up until we can return him to his people. He is not worthy to fight alongside the Mer."

Your ruthless determination has turned your closest ally against you.

Go back to 1.

48

You shake your head. "It's no good. We can't fight an Atlantean battle group all by ourselves and we have no orders. We might get in the way. We must go on to Mer City. Switch to stealth mode."

Reluctantly, Shen does so. In the confusion of

the fighting, you pass through the battle lines unnoticed. A few minutes later, you take the Barracuda into the Mer City docks.

"Come on," says Shen. "We must find my father."

Go to 4.

Admiral Merrow activates a screen and a series of diagrams flash across it.

"That ship is carrying Atlantean cloaking technology far better than our stealth shields," says Merrow grimly. "Our system only confuses long-range sensors. The Atlanteans have found a way to fool close-range detectors, and to make a vessel invisible to all forms of detection — even visual."

You whistle softly. "You mean, you can't even see it?"

"Exactly. Captain Tempest is directing the Atlantean forces from her Nautilus cruiser, and we have no idea where she is!"

"And you want me to find this ship and destroy it?"

Merrow nods. "If we destroy Tempest, the Atlanteans will call off their attack on my city and head back to Atlantis."

"And then we can follow them," you say.

"Yes, but your job will be easier if you can get hold of the cloaking device."

"What does it look like?" you ask.

Ship type –
Nautilus Cruiser –
Tempest's command
ship.

Capacity –
650 crew.

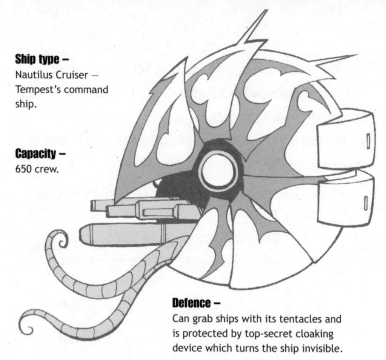

Defence –
Can grab ships with its tentacles and
is protected by top-secret cloaking
device which turns the ship invisible.

Armaments –
Cluster launcher fires a wave
of torpedoes for maximum
damage; tentacles can also
dispatch a range of mines,
depth charges and missiles.

Power system –
Quad jet propulsion
system at rear for
near-silent travel.

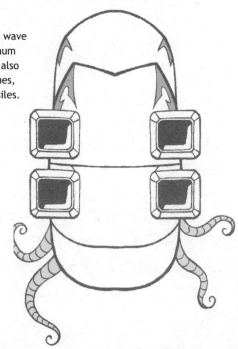

"No one knows — it's a top secret device! But you don't have to go alone. I need Shen here with me, but I have a number of volunteers who are prepared to sail with you in the Barracuda."

If you want to search for Captain Tempest alone, go to 27.

If you wish to accept help from a volunteer, go to 31.

50

You consider your options. "It will take the Brain Coral too long to make copies of the cloaking device," you say at last. "By that time, Shen may be beyond our reach! I have to go now if I'm to have any chance of getting her back — and I have to go alone. The Atlanteans would spot a task force — in the Barracuda, protected by the cloaking device, I may get through."

Admiral Merrow bows to you. "I have misjudged you, human. You are brave — and a good friend. To help you defeat the Atlanteans I will give you one of our most powerful weapons. It is a seaquake device. My people will stow it on your ship and show you how to use it. I'm also giving you a Mer DPV — a Diver Propulsion Vehicle — in case you need extra transport for Shen."

You nod thanks.

Before long, you are alone in the Barracuda, speeding towards the bottom of the ocean. You have the cloaking device and are searching for the entrance to Atlantis. You miss Shen, but you are on your own now. You know you must rescue her, but ORCA are depending on you to close the hole in the ocean floor and stop Triton, King of Atlantis. You only hope you'll be able to do both.

You are a hero! You have saved Mer City...

...but now your toughest challenge lies ahead!

TOP SECRET: Barracuda – sub-aqua bike

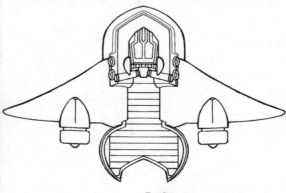

Design –
Intended for short-range travel. Hard for enemies to detect it on scanners because of its streamlined shape.

Armament –
Sea dart missiles.

TOP SECRET: ORCA weapons technology

Urchin mine –
High-explosive charge that can be fixed to a target and set to detonate by timer or motion sensor.

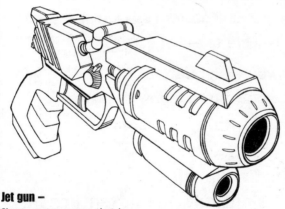

Jet gun –
Short-range weapon that is capable of firing barbed projectiles underwater. Also has a launcher that can fire flares, and self-propelled stun and high explosive grenades.

You have been searching for a way into New Atlantis for some time. You know that unless you manage to locate the hole in the sea floor, Shen will be lost forever.

Suddenly the Barracuda's computer voice breaks the silence. "Atlantean vessel two kilometres ahead."

A 3D image fills the screen. It is a Starfish cruiser, a powerful ship, armed with many explosive spines. You know that the Barracuda's new cloaking device means that the enemy will not be able to see you.

If you wish to attack the cruiser, go to 16.

If you wish to follow it, go to 37.

Continue the adventure in:

ATLANTIS QUEST 4

ATLANTIS ASSAULT

I HERO
DECIDE YOUR OWN DESTINY
ATLANTIS QUEST
ATLANTIS ASSAULT
EDGE
Steve Barlow - Steve Skidmore

About the 2Steves

"The 2Steves" are
Britain's most popular
writing double act
for young people,
specialising in comedy
and adventure. They
perform regularly in schools and libraries,
and at festivals, taking the power of words
and story to audiences of all ages.

Together they have written many books,
including the *Crime Team* and *iHorror* series.

About the illustrator: Jack Lawrence

Jack Lawrence is a successful freelance
comics illustrator, working on titles such as
A.T.O.M., Cartoon Network, *Doctor Who
Adventures*, *2000 AD*, *Gogos Mega Metropolis*
and *Spider-Man Tower of Power*. He also works
as a freelance toy designer.

Jack lives in Maidstone in Kent with
his partner and two cats.

Have you completed the other I HERO Quests?

Battle with aliens in Tyranno Quest:

978 1 4451 0875 9 pb
978 1 4451 1345 6 ebook

978 1 4451 0876 6 pb
978 1 4451 1346 3 ebook

978 1 4451 0877 3 pb
978 1 4451 1347 0 ebook

978 1 4451 0878 0 pb
978 1 4451 1348 7 ebook

Defeat the Red Queen in Blood Crown Quest:

978 1 4451 1499 6 pb
978 1 4451 1503 0 ebook

978 1 4451 1500 9 pb
978 1 4451 1504 7 ebook

978 1 4451 1501 6 pb
978 1 4451 1505 4 ebook

978 1 4451 1502 3 pb
978 1 4451 1506 1 ebook

Also by the 2Steves...

A millionaire is found at his luxury island home – dead! But no one can work out how he died. You must get to Skull Island and solve the mystery before his killer escapes.

The daughter of a Hong Kong businessman has been kidnapped. You must find her, but who took her and why? You must crack the case, before it's too late!

You must solve the clues to stop a terrorist attack in London. But who is planning the attack, and when will it take place? It's a race against time!

An armoured convoy has been attacked in Moscow and hundreds of gold bars stolen. But who was behind the raid, and where is the gold? Get the clues – get the gold.